This book belongs to

Dillon

Useful words

house

hill   ## bike   ## hedge

head   ## doctor

Grey letters represent silent letters.

hospital

ambulance

nurse

plaster

grapes

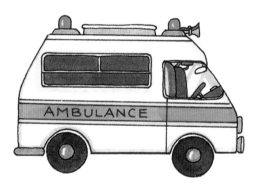

Hairy Hat Man
Goes to hospital

Moira Andrew

Hairy Hat Man hurried up the hill to his house. He was humming to himself and feeling very happy.

Suddenly, Bouncy Ben came whizzing round the corner on his new blue bike.

"Look out!" shouted Ben.

Hairy Hat Man tried to get out of the way.

But it was too late. Hairy Hat Man fell into the hedge.

"I'm ever so sorry," said Ben. "Did you hurt yourself?"

Ben held out his paw to help Hairy Hat Man up.

"Ow!" yelled Hairy Hat Man holding up his hand. "That hurts." he said.

Ben helped the Hat Man up the hill to his house.

Ticking Tess came to make a ham sandwich for the Hat Man. But he wasn't hungry. His head felt hot and heavy.

Tess telephoned for the doctor.

The doctor came and looked

at Hairy Hat Man's hand.

"You need to go to hospital,"

she said.

An ambulance took Hairy Hat Man to hospital.

"You have broken two bones," said the nurse. "We will put your hand in plaster."

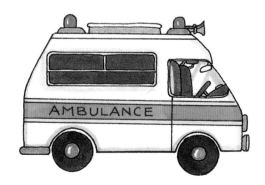

"Now my head hurts as well,"
Hairy Hat Man said to the nurse.

"Take off your hat and let me have
a look at your head," he said.

"You have got a nasty big bump on your head," said the nurse. "You will need to stay in hospital for a day or two."

Then the nurse gave Hairy Hat Man something to make him sleep.

When he woke up, Harry asked if he could go home.

"No, not just yet," said the nurse.

Hairy Hat Man tried to eat some lunch, but he still wasn't very hungry. So he just had a hot drink and went back to sleep.

The Letterlanders were sorry
to hear that the Hat Man was
in hospital.

At visiting time, Golden Girl came
with some grapes. Bouncy Ben
came with some biscuits.

When Hairy Hat Man was well again, Clever Cat came to take him home in her car.

"Don't forget your hat!" called the nurse. And watch out for Bouncy Ben, next time!"

The Letterlanders

Annie Apple **Bouncy Ben** **Clever Cat** **Dippy Duck** **Eddy Elephant** **Fireman Fred** **Golden Girl**

Hairy Hat Man **Impy Ink** **Jumping Jim** **Kicking King** **Lucy Lamp Lady** **Munching Mike**

Naughty Nick **Oscar Orange** **Poor Peter** **Quarrelsome Queen** **Robber Red** **Sammy Snake** **Ticking Tess**

Uppy Umbrella **Vase of Violets** **Wicked Water Witch** **Max and Maxine** **Yellow Yo-yo Man** **Zig Zag Zebra**

This edition produced for
The Book People Ltd., Hall Wood Avenue,
Haydock, St. Helens WA11 9UL

Published by Collins Educational
An imprint of HarperCollins*Publishers* Ltd
77-85 Fulham Palace Road
London W6 8JB

First published 1998

ISBN 0 00 303408 9

British Library Cataloguing in Publication Data
A catalogue record for this book is available from the British Library.

Written by Moira Andrew
Illustrated by Sara Silcock
Designed by Michael Sturley and Sally Boothroyd
Consultant: Lyn Wendon, originator of Letterland

Printed by Printing Express, Hong Kong